ADA RUE
and the
BANISHED

KEREEN GETTEN
ILLUSTRATED BY **SIMONE DOUGLAS**

BLOOMSBURY EDUCATION
LONDON OXFORD NEW YORK NEW DELHI SYDNEY

BLOOMSBURY EDUCATION
Bloomsbury Publishing Plc
50 Bedford Square, London, WC1B 3DP, UK
29 Earlsfort Terrace, Dublin 2, Ireland

BLOOMSBURY, BLOOMSBURY EDUCATION and the Diana logo
are trademarks of Bloomsbury Publishing Plc

First published in Great Britain in 2023 by Bloomsbury Publishing Plc

A catalogue record for this book is available from the British Library

ISBN: PB: 978-1-8019-9129-2; ePDF: 978-1-8019-9127-8; ePub: 978-1-8019-9128-5

2 4 6 8 10 9 7 5 3 1

Text design by Sarah Malley

Printed and bound by CPI Group (UK) Ltd, Croydon, CR0 4YY

MIX
Paper | Supporting
responsible forestry
FSC
www.fsc.org   FSC® C171272

To find out more about our authors and books visit www.bloomsbury.com
and sign up for our newsletters

⋅∗⋅∗⋅ CONTENTS ∗⋅∗⋅∗⋅

✦·✦·✦ CHAPTER ONE ✦·✦·✦

Two boxes of books and three boxes of clothes sit in the garage next to a hundred more boxes for the rest of the house. All with words scribbled on them in Mum's funny handwriting: *For the Living Room, For the Office, Ada's room.*

I stand between the boxes feeling empty. It's official. We are here. There is no going back.

This morning I woke hoping Mum and Dad had changed their minds. That the goodbye cards and presents we received from neighbours and family would make them want to stay.

I thought maybe it would make them sad enough to stay in the city with the people we knew and not move to the middle of nowhere where I would have to start all over again.

When I walked downstairs this morning in our old flat, I was praying everything would be back in its place – the sofa, the photos, the TV – but instead the rooms were still empty, and Dad was packing the last of our things into our two cars. My heart had sunk, but I hadn't given up hope, not completely. Anything could still happen. A meteor could hit earth, or one of the cars could get a flat tyre, or the new school Mum was going to work at could evaporate and disappear. I've seen it in the movies, so why couldn't it happen in real life?

The door inside the garage that leads into our new house is open and I can hear Mum shouting instructions to Dad.

"The pans go in the kitchen, Lloyd; you should know that."

"I thought the pans went in the laundry room," Dad shouts back. He chuckles at his own joke.

The garage door is still open from when the removal men carried all the furniture and boxes from their lorry into the house. Now the red brick driveway is empty and silent.

Dad's black Range Rover, that Mum bought for his fortieth birthday, sits on the pavement and Mum's old banger, as Dad calls it, is behind.

A kid not much younger than me sits on his bike across the road staring at me. I spotted him out of the living room window, and he hasn't moved since, not even when I stepped into the garage and stared back. His bike is tilted, his left foot on the ground, his right on the peddle, and his helmet is too big for him – it almost covers his eyes. Like it was a hand-me-down from his older brother that doesn't fit him yet.

Mum pops her head into the garage. "You going to pick one of those boxes up or stand there all day?" she asks, adjusting her head scarf to cover the front of her hair. Her skin is shiny from sweat and her white vest has marks on it from carrying furniture inside. She had muttered to herself earlier that wearing white was a bad idea and what was she thinking.

"Mum," I say, pointing to the boy on the other side of the street. Mum leans further out to get a better look, then steps into the garage with only a pair of slippers covering her feet. She stands next to me with her hands on her hips.

"Hello!" she calls out to the boy. "Are you our new neighbour?" She uses her 'teacher voice' as Dad calls it. Her high-pitched sing-song voice that makes her sound happier than she actually is.

The boy straightens his bike and rides off without saying anything. I hope he's hasn't gone to tell his friends that a weird family have moved in. I hope he's just late for his lunch or something.

Mum frowns then shakes her head. "Hmm," she mutters, heading back into the house, "maybe he's shy."

I know what shy is, it's what everyone calls me because I don't say much, but he didn't seem shy, he just seemed strange. Like he was watching us except I don't know why.

Mum glances back at me, "Hurry up with those boxes, Ada, they won't unpack themselves."

I'm still thinking about the strange boy on his bike when I pick up a box filled with books. It's so heavy I almost fall backwards.

"Whoa!" Dad grabs the box from me. "Alright Tarzan," he says, "why don't you grab one of the lighter ones."

I pick up a lighter box and follow him into the kitchen, past the island with white stools around it, down the gangway with framed photos leaning on the floor ready to be put on the wall, and up the winding carpet stairs to the first-floor landing. Dad adjusts the box, takes a breath then continues up the other set of stairs to the loft where my room is.

The final stair is short; he has to stand on the step below and nudge the door open with his foot before stepping into the room. He drops the box on the floor. "Phew," he cries, wiping his forehead.

I place my box next to his on the grey carpet. The room is empty apart from a bed frame against the wall. The mattress leans next to it and to the left of the bed is a built-in white wardrobe. Mum has ordered a new chest of drawers and a desk for me that matches the wardrobe, because this room is ten times bigger than my old one at the flat, but they haven't arrived yet.

"You're one lucky girl," Dad says looking around, "I would have loved a loft when I was your age." It's the third time he's said that. He said it when we first came to look at the house. He said it again when we arrived this morning before the removal truck. It's as if he's trying to convince me that I will be happy here. That it will be just as good as the city, but I know it won't. How could it be?

He doesn't wait for me to answer because I don't usually. Mum and Dad are so used to me not saying anything, I don't think they even notice anymore. But what I want to say is, I would swap this house for our tiny city flat any day. I would swap this for the constant sounds of fire engines and loud music, of neighbours screaming and the dotted lights across the city at night shining through the thin curtains.

"Right," he says turning towards the door, "five hundred more boxes to go! Come on, let's see if we can get this done by six, then we can play Monopoly and steal all your Mum's properties."

It's our favourite game to play, and we play it every Saturday night. Dad and I always team up against Mum because she gets so into it. It's funny to see how upset she gets when we steal houses from her.

An hour later, Mum sends Dad for lunch, and he takes me with him. "Might as well see what we're dealing with in this town," he says. "Your grandpa has left three messages already asking us to change our minds." Dad chuckles getting into the car, "Who knew he would miss us so much?" He starts the engine, "Right, let's go explore."

Dad was born in the city; he's never lived anywhere else just like I haven't. He says he's excited to see what it's like to live in a small town.

But I think it's easier for him being an adult. He won't have to start a new school like I will when the summer holidays are over. He won't have to listen to more people asking him why he's so quiet. He won't have to wait for people to get used to him all over again like I will.

We drive out of our quiet cul-de-sac with single houses on either side all looking exactly the same; red-brick two-storey homes with sloping driveways.

We come to the end of the road at a junction and Dad clicks the left indicator, but I wish he had clicked right and driven us back home where everyone knows me as quiet Ada and doesn't care.

We drive along an empty road and enter the centre of Littleton looking for a supermarket, but all we find is a grocery store, a butchers and a repair shop all next to each other. The roads are quiet, not like back home in the city where there is noise even when you go to sleep. There are hardly any people either, and we only spot two cars on the road.

When we enter the grocery store, the man behind the counter looks up and for a minute he just stares at us, but Dad doesn't seem to notice. Or maybe he does because he takes my hand, and he only does that when we're crossing the street, or he thinks I might be in danger.

We walk down the aisle – it's cold from the air con, which at first feels nice from the 'random British heat' as Mum calls it, but then it gets too cold, and I snuggle up next to Dad.

I think though it's because of the cold stare the man behind the counter is giving us. I can see him in the mirror on the ceiling.

Dad picks up a few things to make sandwiches and takes it to the counter where the man is still staring. He's bald and his head is shiny from the sun coming through the window. I keep my eyes fixed on his head, so I don't have to look into his eyes.

"Just these please," Dad says, taking out his wallet

which forces me to let go, so I grab my left arm with my right hand instead.

The man rings up the food. "New around here?" he asks as his head tilts towards the till.

"First day," Dad says in his usual happy voice that seems so loud in this small shop. He sways on his heels, "My wife got a job as a teacher; she wanted to try working for a small school instead of the big city ones." The shop falls silent except for the ring of the till.

"She's a small-town girl," Dad adds because he doesn't like silence. "She was born on the islands."

The man looks up, his eyebrows raised "Jersey?"

Dad laughs loudly as though it's the funniest joke he's ever heard, "No… no… Jamaica."

My eyes move from the shopkeeper's head to his face to see his reaction. Some people act strange when you tell them your Mum is from another country, but he doesn't react at all.

He must be good at hiding his feelings, like I am. I've become good at hiding how I feel, it stops people from asking questions that I don't want to answer because answering forces me to talk. My body feels all funny when I'm forced to speak to people, especially strangers. I get all shaky, my brain goes blank, and the words don't come quickly enough.

Dad notices a sign on the window and points to it nudging me. I follow his finger to the sign asking for a newspaper boy or girl.

"What do you think?" he says to me. "You can earn some pocket money and it will get you out of the house." I shrink back shaking my head frantically but stop when I notice the man looking at me. I don't want him to think I'm rude, so I change my head shaking to a hesitant nod.

"That position still open?" Dad asks the man behind the counter.

He nods, handing Dad the bag. "The kids round here don't want to do any hard work," he says, "it's been there for a while." He turns to me, "You got a bike?" I give a barely there nod. The man looks at Dad, "She speak?" he asks.

Dad laughs and hands over the money, but it's not the sort of laugh that means he finds it funny, it's the sort of laugh he does when he can't believe what he's heard. "She speaks when it's necessary," he says, and he wraps his arm around my shoulder.

14

The man doesn't seem impressed, "Well all she needs is a bike, it's a small town so it won't take her long. A bunch of houses in the morning, that's all. If she can start tomorrow, it will help me out, so I don't have to keep closing the shop."

Dad looks at me and I plead with my eyes. "Why don't we discuss it with Mum?" he suggests. He smiles at the man who doesn't smile back, "We'll give you a call this evening."

When we leave the shop, Dad nudges me, "Look at that, we've been here less than a day and you already have a job offer. How cool is that?"

I feel something on the back of my neck and turn to see the man in the store watching us from his shop window. As I turn back to Dad a weird feeling comes over me and I glance across the road.

It's the boy on the bike. The one who was outside our house watching us, just like the man in the store. Something doesn't feel right about this town, but I don't say anything to Dad, not yet, not until I know for sure what it is.

✴⋆✴ CHAPTER TWO ✴⋆✴

"Ada... Ada wake up." I feel someone ruffling my shoulders and pull away, burying my head into the pillow.

"Come on sleepy head," Dad's voice reaches me even when I cover my ears. "It's time to get up. You don't want to be late for your first paper round, do you?"

I do actually. I want to be so late that the strange man at the store changes his mind about hiring me so I don't have to get up this early or, more importantly, I don't have to speak to the strange man.

I had hoped Mum would say no when Dad told her about the paper round at dinner yesterday. We sat around the small table with boxes at our feet. I had stared really hard at her while she considered what Dad was telling her. In my head I had wished her to say no. I focused so hard on her that I gave myself a headache. But it was no use, she agreed with Dad, it would be a great way for me to make friends.

I roll over on to my back realising Dad isn't going to leave. I glare at him through sleepy eyes. He chuckles. "Why you look so mad?" he says as he walks over to the door. "Meet me downstairs in ten minutes. You don't want to be late on your first day, it creates a bad impression."

He leaves the door open knowing I would have to get up to close it. I sigh staring at the ceiling. So we're still here then. It wasn't a dream. We really have moved to the middle of nowhere.

It's light outside, even though it's six a.m. Dad is his usual chirpy self as we get into the car and he turns the engine on.

"Isn't this exciting, Ada?" he says as the car rolls off the driveway and into the cul-de-sac.

It doesn't take long for us to reach the store. My heart sinks when Dad parks outside. The street is empty, but the shutters are up in the shop, and there is a sign saying 'OPEN'.

Dad turns in his seat but doesn't turn off the engine. "This is where I leave you," he says.

My eyes widen, "You're leaving me?"

He laughs, stroking my shoulder, "You didn't think I was going to do the paper round with you, did you?"

I turn back to the window, staring at the store. No, but I at least expected him to come inside with me. I close my eyes momentarily, trying to talk myself into it. *There's nothing you can do about it now, Ada.*

Dad gets out of the car and unhooks my bike from the roof, rolling it on to the pavement.

I sigh, dragging myself out. He hands me the bike and helmet before getting back into the car. The window rolls down. A look of worry crosses his face. "I'll see you at home," he says with a weak smile, "eight a.m. on the dot." He pulls away before I can say anything, spinning the car round on the empty road and driving off.

I stand outside the shop, staring at the door for what seems like forever, before mustering up the courage to push it open. The bell over the door rings, and the shopkeeper looks up from behind the counter. He has a pile of newspapers and is folding each one, before placing them into a bright yellow bag. He doesn't say anything as I walk over to him hesitantly. I stop in front of the counter staring at the newspapers, so I don't have to look into his eyes.

"These are your deliveries for the day," he says, placing the last newspaper in the bag and handing it to me over the counter. I take it from him and put it over my shoulder. He hands me a piece of paper. "These are the addresses; you have a phone?" I take my phone out of my pocket to show him. He nods, "Put the addresses in, and you should find them easy. It's a small town so you shouldn't get lost." I glance over the piece of paper, trying to hide how frightened I am at getting this wrong.

"Well, go on then," he says waving me away, "they won't deliver themselves."

I spin on my heels in a mild panic that I've already done something wrong.

I yank the door open and rush outside, grateful to be out of there. As I grab my bike, I turn to look behind me and he's watching me from the window. I jump on the seat of the bike peddling away as fast as I can.

..*.*.*.*.

It feels strange riding through the town centre with no one around. I soon forget about the shopkeeper as I take in my new surroundings. I come to a clock set on a small roundabout. To the left is a pebbled road for pedestrians that leads to a small market with empty stalls. I look right then left, and ride straight over to the other side. A gentle summer breeze blows against my face, and I relax into the seat happy not to see anyone around.

In the distance, I can see a small cottage. I slow down as I approach. It's a bungalow, surrounded by a short fence and a wooden gate. Dropping the bike on to the grass, I check the list. Mrs Abel.

The curtains are still drawn. I open the gate and walk down the stone steps to the black front door. There is a Christmas wreath hanging over the door even though Christmas was eight months ago. I flatten the newspaper, pushing it through the letterbox before hurrying back to my bike.

There are four more houses along the same road, all with people who require newspapers. First is Errol Clay, who lives in a small white cottage surrounded by lush gardens with pink and white flowers. Then

20

there is Mr and Mrs Nassar, who live in a much bigger house than Mrs Abel. Their house is new, painted white, with two floors and a gravelled driveway. They have a dog that barks so loudly, it takes me five minutes to post their newspaper because I think my hand is going to be bitten off.

Then there is Mr Pillock who has a really old car outside his house. He is in his garage working on another car, but he doesn't see or hear me because his radio is playing too loudly. I slip past him and post the paper before riding off at top speed.

The last house on this road is on the corner. It's an old farmhouse with a steeple-like roof and tall trees towering over it. But it isn't the house that catches my attention, it's the field straight ahead at the end of the road. I press the brakes sharply outside the farmhouse. The field goes on for miles, but something doesn't look quite right. I roll my bike closer. It is as if there is a thick fog in the middle of the field. Nowhere else. I drop my bike to the ground, edging towards it slowly, checking the sky – no fog. The sky is a clear light blue with hardly any clouds. I look behind me, down the road where I came from. It's all clear. The sun is shining down on the tarmacked road. I turn back to the field and step forward, hesitantly.

"Hello there!" I jump spinning round to see a man standing outside the farmhouse, his hands on his hips.

He glances down at the bright yellow bag sitting across my shoulder. "Do you have something for me?" he asks.

I hurriedly grab a newspaper and rush over, handing it to him. He glances over it, then at me.

"So you're our new newspaper girl," he says. I don't know if it's a question but I nod anyway.

"And what's your name?" he asks.

I clear my throat, "Ada... Ada Rue." My voice comes out small and I cringe a little inside.

He offers me his hand, "Ada, I'm the mayor of this town, nice to meet you."

My mouth falls open as he takes my limp hand and shakes it. I've never met a mayor before. Dad will be so impressed! He turns and heads back into his house, and I don't move until he's shut his front door.

I pick up my bike, turn it around and jump on, cycling back into town totally forgetting about the fog in the field.

CHAPTER THREE

It's another sunny day. I sit on my bike and peddle slowly down the drive. I catch a glimpse of that boy again, watching me from his bedroom window. So he does live across from me! I think about waving but he's staring so hard that I think he can't be friendly and ride away.

When I arrive at the shop, the shopkeeper has left the bag out for me, and the newspapers to fold.

I don't need the addresses this time, but I take the list anyway, folding it into my pocket. I ride out of town and alongside the green fields. Now I know I won't bump into anyone on my round, I start to enjoy my morning ride.

I slip in my ear pods and play my favourite playlist. I settle into the seat, my elbows relaxed, my feet turning the pedals to the rhythmic beat.

A few minutes later I reach Mrs Abel's cottage, where I push the newspaper through the letterbox.

I head back to my bike and continue to Errol's, then on to Mr and Mrs Nassar's. I deliver their paper and head to Mr Pillock's house. Just like yesterday, the radio is playing and his garage is open. I slip by him to the front door, deliver the newspaper and sneak away before he spots me. Then I head to the mayor's house.

As I ride up to the mayor's gate, my eyes travel to the field again. The fog is still there, only this time it seems to be breathing, like a heartbeat. I pedal past the mayor's house and over to the field, where I drop my bike and slip down the embankment, edging gingerly towards the fog. The closer I get, the more it seems like an everlasting wall that goes on forever. My feet stop in front of the fog, and I stare at it in awe.

I lean my head back, my eyes following it to where it meets the sky.

With my heart in my mouth, I raise my hand to touch the fog. The palm of my hand goes through it like air. I withdraw my hand quickly with a gasp. Curiosity gets the better of me and I gently push my hand in again, then my wrist, then my arm, then it is as if something grabs me from the other side, and my entire body is sucked through.

Inside the fog, my heartbeat echoes, loud and clear. I can barely catch my breath, the air is so thick. I can just about make out my fingers. I walk in further to see how far it goes and, in the distance, I see a blur of figures. I edge towards them, expecting to see the mayor asking me where his paper is. I take another few steps, then the fog ends and I am in a clearing. But this is no ordinary clearing. I take a sharp intake of breath.

This is another world.

Here, the blue sky is now dark grey, almost black. The green field looks silver, like the decorations you put on Christmas trees, and standing very still is a boy blinking back at me. He looks very much like the boy on the bike who lives on my road, but this boy has pixie ears and emerald green eyes. He starts to make a frantic sound with his mouth, like a shrill whistle, his eyes not leaving me. Within seconds strange-looking people appear from all sides; some tall, some small, one with a tail, another with red skin. They all gather next to the boy looking back at me with the same expression the boy has – bewilderment.

I take a sudden step back almost tripping over a stone in the ground.

"No, wait!" a voice says.

A tall woman steps out of the group. She has yellow eyes and green locs that fall down her back. She smiles at me gently. "Don't be afraid," she says and her voice is soothing, like the ripples of a river. I stop, clasping my hands behind my back, twisting my fingers together where they can't be seen.

She moves forward and reaches out her hand, "My name is Miranda, what's yours?"

I look from her to the others. The silence is deafening but my heart is loud against my chest.

She takes another step towards me, "Please," she says reaching for me, her eyes looking desperate. "Please," she begs again. I look into her pleading eyes, then behind me at the foggy wall. I turn back to her and take a small step towards her.

"Ada," I reply in a small voice.

Her hand drops to her side and she lets out a sigh of relief. "Nice to meet you, Ada."

.·.·*.·*.·*.

Miranda takes me by the hand and leads me through a series of huts. Dark wooden huts that are so small I think there must only be one room inside. All the huts are identical, with triangle-shaped roofs and dark wooden doors. The crowd follow closely, not making a sound.

We emerge into an opening where a large fire is burning. The crowd gather around the fire, sitting on stone seats. Miranda sits on a moon-shaped seat at the front and pats the space next to her.

She takes my hand in hers and it is soft, like my pillow back home. I feel a sudden surge of panic. Home! The newspapers! I will be in so much trouble.

"Ada, how did you find us?" Miranda asks gently.

I look around at all the curious faces then back at her. "The fog," I reply quietly. There are murmurs amongst the crowd.

"You saw the fog?" she asks. I nod nervously, my head still trying to grasp where I am and how I got here.

"And then what?" she asks.

"I walked through it," I tell her. The crowd erupts. There are cheers, whoops of excitement and questions thrown at me.

How did I see the fog? Where did I come from? Who am I? Did anyone else see me go into the fog?

I look around me confused and a little frightened. Miranda strokes my hand. "It's okay," she reassures me, "they're happy to see you."

I frown, "Why?"

"Because," she says squeezing my hand, her eyes dancing, "you are the only one out there who can see us."

CHAPTER FOUR

"We were once part of the very town you live in,"
Miranda explains. "We lived next door to all
the people you see out there. We went to school with
them, worked with them, had birthday parties
with them." She sighs, shaking her head, "That was a
wonderful time, for all of us. But then John Crow
became mayor. John is the same as us, but we
constantly locked heads. We wanted to heal people,
make life better with our magic, but he didn't agree."

29

"Why wouldn't he want you to make things better?" I whisper.

"Because he's evil!" someone shouts from the crowd, and suddenly the silence is broken again with chatter. Miranda holds her hand up to silence them, her eyes not leaving mine.

"Because he couldn't make money. If we healed the sick, then who would pay for medicine? He wanted us to be a tourist attraction. To perform for outsiders. He wanted to turn us into a circus act and we refused. So he stole our book of magic and used the spell we never use, a spell only meant for emergencies, the spell of banishment. He sent us here, behind the wall of fog, away from those we love, where no one can see us or the fog, and we cannot see outside. Until you, Ada; until you found us."

I try to digest everything she has told me. The fog, the magic, the evil mayor who I thought was okay when I met him yesterday. My mind flitters from one thought to the next, not knowing what to do, or what to say.

"So can you help us?" someone shouts, breaking the silence.

I feel a sense of panic overcoming me. "Help you do what?" I ask Miranda. She lets go of my hand

and stands. I watch as she walks away, not knowing whether to follow her or stay. She disappears into one of the huts and reappears minutes later with something in her hand. She approaches and extends her hand towards me. She is holding a pile of letters, all wrapped together with string. I look at the letters, then at her blankly.

"We write to our families and our friends," she says softly. "Every day we try different magic to get the letters to them, to let them know we are safe, but our magic is useless in here. This spell that the mayor put on us was designed to hide us. To make sure no one can get access to us, so nothing we try ever gets through the fog." She wraps my hands around the envelopes, "Can you deliver our letters, Ada?"

..*.*.*.

The crowd gather beside the fog as I pack the letters into my yellow newspaper bag. I look over my shoulder at them and they are waving, some with tears in their eyes, some smiling, others probably worrying that I may not even make it back out.

I face the fog and take a deep breath before stepping into it. The thick cloud engulfs me, as it did when I first entered. I can barely see in front of me, except for a tiny light ahead. I follow the light slowly, then start to run as panic rises inside me that I may not get out. I feel a sudden force pushing me out of the fog. I emerge on the other side, falling on to the ground. I sit up staring at the fog; it's still there. I check my bag to see if the letters made it. They did, so I jump to my feet and run up the embankment towards my bike.

I am out of breath when I reach home. I drop my bike in the driveway and rush into the house through the garage and into the kitchen where Mum is making her morning coffee.

"All done already?" she asks. I rush past her, up the stairs and straight into Dad coming out of the bathroom.

"Whoa there! Who's chasing you?" he laughs. I rush by him up the stairs into the loft and shut the door behind me. I throw the newspaper bag on the floor and slide to the ground bringing my knees up to my chin.

I think about Miranda, and all the others behind the fog. I think about how dull and grey it was there, how sad it is that they are stuck there because of the mayor. I think about how I never wanted to do this paper round in the first place. As my breathing slows, I glance over at the bag on the floor. The bag with all the letters.

I crawl on all fours until I am right over the bag. I sit down on my legs and peer inside. The letters are still there. I wasn't dreaming. I take the letters out gingerly, holding them in the palms of my hands, before placing them back inside.

Throwing the bag over my shoulder, I make my way back down the stairs. In the kitchen, Dad is at the breakfast table with his porridge reading a book, and Mum is meditating on the patio outside.

Dad looks up from his book when I enter the kitchen, "You want something to eat?" he asks.

I shake my head not stopping, "I still have some deliveries," I tell him, heading to the garage.

"Really?" he cries out after me. "Why did you come home then?"

I don't answer. Instead, I make my way down the driveway where I left my bike. I reach into the bag and take out a letter, then jump on my bike and start riding.

The first place I stop at is an old two-storey building that looks as though it's been there since the beginning of time. It's on the outskirts of town, just as you turn off my road as though you're heading to the store. The old house, now turned into flats, is painted black, with white railings. I look down at the letter. Apartment four. I climb the steps to the front door and knock. No answer. I turn the handle and it opens into a dark hall. I walk inside checking the numbers until I come to apartment four. I look for the letterbox but there isn't one, so I slip the letter under the door and leave quickly.

There are ten letters in all. Some with familiar names like Mr Pillock, Mr and Mrs Nassar and the shopkeeper Mr Bell, but there are some I don't know, like Miya Hammond and Tyson Diya. Eventually I have just two letters left to deliver. I lean my bike against the streetlamp and enter the store where Mr Bell the shopkeeper is standing behind the till counting money. He glances up as the doorbell rings. I approach the counter, my heart beating fast as I take the bag off my shoulder.

"Drop it round there," he mumbles nodding to behind the counter. I walk around the counter gingerly and place the bag on the floor. Holding the last two letters tightly in my hand, I wait for him to finish what he is doing. Finally, he places the money inside the till and closes it. I thrust the letter at him, then turn on my heels escaping out of the door.

There is one more letter to deliver and it's on my road. When I reach Ballmore Street where I live, I try to find the house number on the letter; number 67. When I find it, I realise not only is it across the road from my house, but it's the same house where the strange boy lives.

As I walk up the driveway, I get that same feeling again. The feeling that I am being watched. I look up to the top window and sure enough he's there, watching me as though he knows when I'll be at his house. I shudder, push the letter through the letterbox, then quickly leave. As I cross the road, I hear a noise and reluctantly turn. The boy is standing in the doorway with the letter in his hand staring back at me, expressionless. I pick up my bike, walk stiffly up my driveway and into the garage, quickly pressing the button that closes the garage door – only then do I let out a sigh of relief.

When the alarm wakes me the next morning, something feels different. I sit up suddenly wondering if I missed my paper round. I grab my phone off the bedside table to check the time. No, I haven't missed it, I'm right on time. I slip out of bed and over to the bedroom door. I open it and listen. Silence. Something feels off; I can't put my finger on what it is, but I get dressed anyway.

Downstairs in the kitchen a bowl of dry cereal is laid out for me.

"Morning!" Mum calls from the living room where she is doing her stretches.

"Morning," I reply, leaving the kitchen and entering the garage. I pick my bike off the wall and open the garage door to a crowd gathered on our driveway. I stop abruptly, my heart pounding. Someone emerges from the crowd and walks towards me; it's Mr Bell, the shopkeeper. He looks frantic which makes me even more scared because he only ever looks calm and a little bit rude sometimes.

"Ada," he says breathlessly, holding the letter in his hand, "we need to talk, but not here. Can we come in?"

"What's going on?" I hear Mum's voice behind me. I turn relieved to see her. She walks towards me still in her gym shorts and sweaty T-shirt. I feel her arm around my shoulders. "What's going on?" she asks again, but this time her voice is sharp.

Mr Bell turns to Mum, "Please," he begs, "can we do this inside? It's not safe out here."

I feel my stomach flip and move closer to Mum.

Mr Bell closes the garage door when everyone is inside. We are plunged into darkness forcing Mum to turn on the light. The commotion brings Dad down, still in his pyjamas.

He looks to Mum confused, "What's going on?" he asks. Mum shrugs her shoulders turning to the small group.

Mr Bell steps forward and so does Dad. They meet in front of me and shake hands.

"We came about the letters," Mr Bell explains to him. Dad glances over his shoulder at Mum who shrugs again.

"What letters?" Dad asks, confused. Mr Bell glances in my direction. My heart leaps out of my chest.

"Don't they know?" Mr Bell asks me. My head falls to my chest and I stare at the ground shaking my head. When I look back up, both Mum and Dad are glaring at me with raised eyebrows.

Mum rests her hands on her hips and tilts her head, "What letters, Ada?"

CHAPTER FIVE

I'm in so much trouble. I can see it on Mum and Dad's faces as Mr Bell tells them the story of the Banished. Their faces go from confusion to disbelief as he tells the same story the Banished told me yesterday. When he gets to the letter part, where I deliver them to everyone standing in our garage, Mum and Dad's eyes are fixed on me.

"We just want to know how she did it and if she can help us," a lady says from the crowd.

Now Mum tilts her head at the lady, "Help you do what exactly?"

"Contact them," Mr Bell says, looking from Mum to Dad earnestly. "She's the only one that has any contact with them. We thought they had gone forever but Ada has given us new hope."

"Hope for what?" Dad asks.

"Hope of seeing them again," Mr Bell says. "Hope of getting their help to the sick, hope of speaking to our loved ones who we thought we would never see again. Our town has fallen apart since they left. We are a closed community, we can't risk going to other towns with our sick for fear of someone finding out about the Banished."

"But we knew about your town," Mum says confused, "and we lived in the city."

Mr Bell frowns, his eyes darting around. "Did you get a letter?" he asks.

"Yes, we got a letter inviting us to come and look around," she answers.

Mr Bell nods, "That was an invitation. The Banished must have sent it before they were taken. They've been searching for the children of the original Banished for some years. No one comes here without an invitation. We are hidden from the rest of the world."

Dad rubs his face with his hands, then shakes his head slowly. He turns to look at me. "You saw these secret people?"

I nod, twisting my mouth from side to side.

"Show me," Dad says. The crowd suddenly becomes unsettled.

"There's just one problem with that," Mr Bell says.

Dad sighs, rolling his head towards Mr Bell, "What?"

"The mayor will notice if we try to contact them. We can't draw attention to the fact that Ada has this gift. It could mean trouble for all of us. That is why we were all so suspicious when you arrived. We never know who to trust. The mayor has spies everywhere. He will notice."

Dad looks at Mr Bell intently as if digesting what he's said. He turns to me again.

"Ada, take me and your mother to where you saw these people," he says. And this time he is adamant.

* * * * * * *

The group's curiosity gets the better of them, and they decide to risk following me, Mum and Dad in the car, but they stop short of the field knowing the mayor's house is right at the corner. Instead, they wait outside Mr Pillock's house.

"Please give them these," Mr Bell hands me letters. He glances at Mum and Dad, "If you go in of course," he adds quickly. I hold the letters firmly in both my hands, scared in case a slight breeze blows them away.

Mum and Dad walk the rest of the way with me, holding my arms. I take them down the field and towards the now familiar haze. I stop right in front of it.

"This is it," I tell them, nodding towards the wall of fog that meets the sky. They look around confused.

"Where?" Mum asks blankly.

I look at them both, frowning. "There," I say, pointing at the fog.

How could they not see it? It cuts off half the field! They look in front of them, behind them, on the ground, up to the sky. My heart pounds against my chest as I watch them trying to find it.

"You don't see it?" I ask, bewildered. They look at me, desperately shaking their heads. A realisation sets on our faces.

"Show us," Dad says. Mum shakes her head frantically, but Dad lays a hand on her. "Show us,

Ada," he repeats softly. I glance at Mum, worry and fear etched into her face.

"It's okay Mum," I tell her, "they're really nice." I walk towards the fog and then, with one look over my shoulder at their worried faces, I step inside.

..*.*.*.*.

When I walk out of the fog to the other side, the Banished are already waiting for me. It is as though they heard me coming, or maybe with their magic they saw me.

I stand in front of them awkwardly, holding the letters tightly in the grip of my hands until Miranda rushes forward. I am relieved to see her, and she throws her arms around me hugging me so tightly I have to tell her I can't breathe.

She takes my hand in hers and looks over her shoulder. She blows a breath of air into the fog and whispers 'she is safe'. I glance into the wall of fog and see a murky outline of Mum and Dad. Miranda smiles at me, "Now they won't worry," she says, leading me away.

Miranda makes me feel safe but I can't explain why. It could be the way she guides me through the crowd, pushing anyone out of the way who gets too close, or it could be the way her fingers wrap around mine so tightly that I feel I would never lose her. Whatever it is, I feel less afraid next to her.

She leads me to the stone seats and we wait until everyone is sat down before she speaks.

"Our messenger has returned," she announces to the captivated crowd. The air erupts with cheering. She raises her hand to silence them, then turns to me still holding on to my hand. "Ada," she says softly, yet her voice is crystal clear. "We are so lucky to have you. You have been the light we have wished for." She looks down at the letters in my hand, "Do you have something for us?" I nod, holding the letters out to her. There are murmurs as some in the crowd move closer to see.

"And what is this?" she asks me, smiling. I look down at the letters thinking it is pretty obvious.

"The people you wrote to," I explain.

She leans in and whispers, "Louder so they can hear your beautiful voice."

I clear my throat and turn to face the crowd. I feel all their eyes on me, desperately waiting on the edge of their seats. Somehow, I don't feel the jitters that would usually come with speaking. Somehow, I feel calm.

"The people you wrote to," I say as loud as I can. My voice echoes as though I was in a tunnel.

"They wrote back," I explain. Everyone jumps to their feet and rushes towards me. I sink back in fright as Miranda steps in front of me to block the approaching crowd.

"Quiet!" Miranda booms. Her voice is like thunder; it roars into the air like a powerful wind, sending the crowd back to their seats. She lowers her hand slowly until the crowd is completely silent.

"We have talked about this," she says, looking around at the others. "We have prepared for if this was to happen. This is not news to us, we have been waiting for what we knew would eventually come." She moves closer to me. "Now, Ada will call your name, and you will approach, receive your letter and begin the plan. Do not waste time on emotions, do not get distracted. Who knows how much time we have before the mayor finds out – we must act quickly." She nods to me. I look down at the envelopes in my hand and begin to call the names written on the front of each one. Gradually they approach and receive their letters.

Caesar, the first person I met, is a boy of around 16 who has pixie ears. He grins widely, taking his letter with a small bow.

Then there is Doris, Shah, Clay, Ruman, Elis, Abo, Fawn, Boa, and lastly, Miranda. She takes her letter from me and her eyes light up. She stares at the letter intently, then at me. "Thank you, Ada," she says. I watch as they disperse in different directions.

Some find a space on the ground and sit with their legs crossed reading their letters. Others, like Miranda, disappear into their small wooden huts, until I am left standing on my own.

I take in my surroundings for the first time. We are in a forest, even though outside it is a field. Somehow in here things seem different, as though we are in another world. For instance, it's dark. It could be ten p.m., 11, or maybe 12, it's hard to tell with no clocks.

When I check my phone the time has disappeared. Only dotted lines remain on the screen where the time would be. It's as if time stands still here. The huts are all together on one side, and behind me there is an outdoor kitchen with an open pit that has charred wood and smoke coming from it. There is a path that leads away from the huts. Unlike everywhere else the path is lined with pink flowers, the only bright colour around us.

I start to follow the path when a loud sound comes bellowing through the skies. It sounds like a thousand drums coming from all corners of the heavens and I am rooted in fear. I feel someone grab my hand and spin me around. Only then do I notice the panic around me as everyone scrambles, running in different directions.

"Ada, you must go now," Miranda says, leading me through the crowd of panic and over to the wall of fog.

"What is that?" I ask frantically as the noise gets louder, almost deafening. I cover my ear with my spare hand.

"You've been found out," Miranda explains, "the mayor must know you're here. You must go, now!"

I stare at her wide-eyed, my heart thundering against my chest.

Miranda steadies my shaking hand. "Don't be afraid," she says gently, lowering her head to meet mine. "You are more powerful than you know, Ada."

I want to ask her what she means by that but she is already facing the panicking crowd. "Bring your letters," she orders.

"But I haven't written mine yet," Caesar says. "Please," he begs Miranda, "I'll be quick."

Miranda shakes her head, "We don't have time." She glances at their disappointed faces, then takes a deep breath. "Okay, give Ada the breath of words but make it quick. Every second puts her at risk, and those we love."

Caesar runs over to me and places both hands on either side of my head. He rests his forehead on mine. "Breathe in, Ada," he whispers. "One, two... " he inhales deeply, and I do the same. A funny feeling overcomes me. Light headedness, then a feeling of calm.

Tell mother to use the medicine under the stairs. Under the third floorboard with the letter X. Tell her I love her.

A gasp escapes me as he lets go. Then one by one they all do the same. They hold my head, lean theirs against mine so I can feel their breath, then I hear their thoughts without them saying a word. It happens so quickly; I can barely comprehend what is happening until it's over. Then, Miranda rushes me to the wall of fog. "Go," she says urgently and pushes me through.

When I emerge on the outside, the drum sound is just as deafening. Mum is running towards me. "Hurry!" she shouts. I rush towards her and she grabs my hand tightly as we run across the field and on to the embankment. Dad is waiting with the car door open – the crowd have disappeared. Dad speeds off before Mum even has time to close her door.

47

We don't go far. Mr Pillock is waving on the street corner outside his house and Dad spins the car into his drive. Mr Pillock runs ahead of us as Dad follows him to the back of the house and into an open garage big enough for five cars. It's already full with only space left for us. As Dad parks the car Mr Pillock closes the garage door.

We all get out of the car and follow Mr Pillock silently to a corner of the garage where there are rows of shelves filled with knick-knacks. A bicycle wheel, a box filled with tools, overalls, and an old-fashioned lamp which he picks up, clicking a switch underneath. He presses on the shelf right in the centre, then stands back. There is a moment of silence. Mum and Dad exchange looks, then suddenly the shelf begins to move and a hidden door opens. Holding the lamp out in front of him, Mr Pillock descends down some dark stairs. I jump as Dad closes the door behind me. Now the lamp is the only light guiding us.

Every movement echoes as we plunge deeper and deeper, until finally Mr Pillock stops. He shines a light around to reveal another door. Turning the handle, he pushes the door open and we step inside.

CHAPTER SIX *.·*.

The group, who were previously at my house, fill what looks like a basement. Mr Pillock says they call it the Hideaway. "It's where the Banished would hide their families if they ever needed to protect them," he explains. "We don't have their magical powers, so if for any reason they couldn't protect us from someone trying to steal their magic, this was our safe place. It was a constant fear. The world doesn't like different," he sighs. "But the kind of different with magical powers that can change the world? Well, you will always have a target on your back."

The room we stand in is not remarkable. There's nothing magical about it, it's nothing like the world the Banished live in. It is just a large cellar with four tattered brown sofas, some chairs, a small kitchen with a sink against the wall and a door off to the side with a 'Toilet' sign. The walls are white exposed brick, the floor is a dark-red stone and there is one yellow lightbulb hanging from the low ceiling.

Mr Bell turns off the lamp in his hand, and looks around the room at all the faces staring back at us.

"So help me understand," Dad says with his hands on his hips, a deep frown indented in his forehead. "What's the urgency, and what is that noise?"

Everyone's eyes look to the ceiling. "That noise," Mr Bell says gravely, "is our emergency warning. It sounds when the mayor thinks our town is in danger."

Mum moves closer to Dad, still gripping my hand, "In danger of what?" she cries.

"Well," Mr Bell replies, "either your kid's cover has been blown and the mayor knows about her, or… " he glances at the others, then back at Mum and Dad. "Or we really are in danger and the Crawler is back."

Dad's hand slides around Mum's back, "The Crawler?"

"Why don't you sit down and let me make you a cup of tea?" Mrs Abel says, getting up and moving over to the small kitchen against the brick wall. "It's been a long morning for all of us." No one disagrees as she bustles around taking cups out of cupboards. She glances over her shoulder and smiles warmly at Mum and Dad. "Then we will tell you everything," she says, and returns her focus to filling the kettle.

Under the dim light inside the basement they call the Hideaway, Mr Bell grabs a hard-backed wooden chair and places it in the middle of us all. He sits with his hands clasped together on his knees, his feet tilted on to his toes, and tells us the story of the Banished.

"Long ago," Mr Bell says, "way before I was born, when casting magic was against the law and practising it meant death, a group of witches, fleeing from persecution, went on a journey to find safety for themselves and for their future families. They called themselves the Banished. They found Littleton. It was deserted after three consecutive fires and no one had lived there since. People believed it was a cursed town, but the Banished felt drawn there, safe in the knowledge that it was miles away from any other life.

51

Fearful of being found, and wanting to live a normal life, they set a magical wall around the town to stop any intruders getting in, and there they lived happily for many years. They built homes, had families and lived a peaceful life, until they were betrayed. One of their very own, Mocasa, a young man who resented being locked away from the rest of the world, escaped into the night to the nearest town. He persuaded his two best friends, Amron and Kane, to go with him. When they reached the town, Mocasa was tricked by a woman he fell in love with. On learning about Littleton, she persuaded Mocasa to take her there, hungry to have the magic for herself. We do not know if he realised, but the woman planned to take an army with her.

The army hid in the countryside until Mocasa lowered the magical walls, and then they stormed the town. Realising they were surrounded, the leaders cast a spell on all of their children, taking away the magical powers that had plagued their own lives. The leaders perished on that dreadful day but their children, who were no longer magical, were spared. Little did the leaders know that when they took the magical powers away from their children, they did not take them from their children's children.

So we, the children of the Banished, were taken to the city. We were put into children's homes at first, then adopted out to new families, never thinking we would ever see days like these again. When we realised the magical powers had gone to our children, one by one we returned to Littleton, in the hope that it would protect us once again. Only this time, we didn't have the magic to protect our children. It was our children we had to rely on to protect us.

The Banished didn't want to keep the magic for themselves, but we were afraid that history would repeat itself. We are not on any maps, and although many have heard the story of the magical town, we cannot be found except by invitation. Specific instructions are given to those we invite, descendants of the Banished who may not have known about us. Only then do we reveal our town so we can be found."

"Like the letter we received," Mum mumbles.

"As far as most people are concerned, we do not exist. But we don't always get things right. One of the letters we sent was to Mocasa's son, but when he came his intentions weren't pure. He believed we had abandoned his father, that we had made him a scapegoat, and he wanted revenge. Just as Mocasa had exposed us, Mocasa's son wanted to eliminate the Banished. He believed that magic had ruined his family and he wanted revenge in return. We call him the Crawler because after being banned from Littleton, he waits patiently until we reopen the town to let in a new family, and then tries to sneak in."

"What does he want?" Dad asks.

Mr Bell shrugs his shoulders, "Revenge. He wants to destroy the very thing he thinks destroyed his father. We created this Hideaway for safety, but it turns out the danger came from the inside, from the mayor."

"What does the mayor want?" Dad asks, scratching his head.

"He had big plans for the town," Mrs Abel says, warming her hands around her cup of tea. "He wanted to profit from the Banished, make Littleton his Disneyland where people would come to see the Banished perform tricks for a fee, but we refused."

"So the mayor stole the book of magic," I say quietly, remembering what Miranda told me. Everyone turns to me and the room falls silent. "He punished them because they wouldn't do what he wanted, so he stole it and banished them to another place."

"But why didn't the Banished use their magic to stop him?" Dad cries, astounded.

"They can't," a voice says from the back of the room. When I look it's the boy from my road who is always on his bike.

"My name is Grayson and my brother, Caesar, is one of the Banished. He told me there is a spell so strong that they would never use it. The spell creates a wall-like fog and inside the fog they have no magical powers outside. They can't get out."

Dad scoffs, "Why would they use that spell? Seems silly to me."

"It was to protect them from anyone who wanted to take their magic, or if someone was misusing their magic, but one of them had to be on the outside to reverse it." The boy explains.

"We were protecting ourselves from repeating history," Mr Bell adds patiently.

"So if none of the Banished are outside the bubble to reverse it, they're stuck in there forever," Mum says, piecing it together. She shakes her head with a sigh.

"We just never knew where they went," Mrs Abel says. "The spell makes them disappear, and with the mayor having the book, he has complete control over all of us. We didn't want to do anything to upset him in the hope that he would bring the Banished back."

Mum sits forward suddenly, her eyes wide with fear, "So, if you are all descendants of the original Banished, and your children all have magical powers… " her eyes flit to me, "Why Ada?"

I look at Mr Bell and he looks back at me gravely. "Well, we're not a hundred percent sure," he says glancing at the others for support, "but we think she may be the descendant of Amron, Mocasa's best friend."

CHAPTER SEVEN

The room feels heavy as everyone turns to me. There is pity in some of their eyes. *Poor girl,* I imagine them thinking. *Poor girl, related to a traitor.* I shift in my seat, clasping my hands tightly in front of me.

"Amron, one of the people responsible for the death of the original Banished?" Dad cries in disbelief. "No, you're wrong."

"Besides we don't know any Amron," Mum agrees. "He would be my father or my husband's father and neither of them are called Amron."

"We don't believe Amron had anything to do with the Littleton attack," Errol says from the back of the room. "We believe he was there to help his friend if he needed him."

The others nod in agreement.

"It still doesn't make any sense," Mum says frowning, "neither of our fathers are called Amron."

"We think he changed his name to Albert," Mr Bell says. "He wanted to get as far away from his past as possible. He tried to protect the town, but when he realised he could not do it alone, when he saw the children being taken, he fell into the depths of despair and ran as far away from his past as he could get. Maybe he felt at fault, maybe he couldn't face the pain."

I feel a sudden jolt in my stomach, "Dad, isn't grandpa called Albert?"

Dad shakes his head adamantly, "No... yes that is his name but no, it's not him." Mum places her hand on his tapping leg. "He would have said something," Dad cries.

"Lloyd…" Mum says, but Dad continues to shake his head.

"We were close. He would have told me. How could he not tell me?"

"It's possible he never wanted you to know," Mr Bell explains. "He suffered huge guilt after the attack."

Dad gets to his feet and paces the room. We watch in silence as he shakes his head until finally he slumps in his chair, covering his face with his hands.

"This is a lot to take in, I know," Mr Bell says, "but I'm afraid we're going to have to put a pause in this conversation. At least until we find out why the alarm is going off. Grayson is going to see what he can find out."

As Grayson makes his way to the front of the room Mr Bell explains, "The mayor uses Grayson and a few other boys as spies to find out what we know. He has promised to save Grayson's brother if Grayson remains loyal to him. What he doesn't know is that Grayson has been reporting back to us."

"But he's just a kid," Mum says, shaking her head as Grayson puts on his jacket.

"He's a kid with something none of us have," Mr Bell explains. "Grayson's brother gave him the spell of protection from birth. It means he can't be hurt by anyone."

I stand, suddenly remembering the messages I have to relay to them all. I try to push the thought of Grandad Albert out my mind and focus. I spot Mrs Dalton, Caesar's mother.

"Caesar says there is medicine under the stairs," I tell her in a rush of words in case I forget. There is a gasp around the room. "He says it's under the floorboard that has a letter on it."

Mrs Dalton's eyes mist over, "The letter X," she murmurs. "I saw him carving it in the floor. I thought he was misbehaving. I sent him to his room." She sniffs back tears, "Why didn't he tell me?"

"He says he loves you," I tell her quietly, twisting my fingers in front of me.

I turn to Mr and Mrs Nassar who look at me hopefully, holding on to each other. "Ruman and Boa say to tell you not to worry, that they will be with you before you know it."

I turn to each one and retell what the Banished told me as if I was reciting something I have always known. As if this information was always there.

"I need that medicine," Mrs Dalton says. "I have a rare illness. Caesar always knew what to do. Since he's been gone, I've been getting worse and worse. This medicine will save my life."

"I'll get it Mum," Grayson says. He turns to me, "You should come with me, you know exactly where it is."

Mum jumps up, "No, not again, no!"

Dad pulls her back down. "She'll be okay," he says, giving me a nod to leave.

Normally I would be happy Mum wants me to stay where it's safe. I've never liked going out into the unknown. It's scary and gives me the butterflies. But ever since I met the Banished something has changed in me. It's not that I feel more confident, I feel the same, but I know what I have to do and so I'll do whatever it takes to help the Banished because somehow, they remind me of me. I know what it's like to be alone. I know what it's like to feel like you don't belong.

I hurry after Grayson before Mum changes her mind.

CHAPTER EIGHT

Outside it is eerily quiet. Quieter than my early morning paper round before anyone gets up.

"Jump on the back," Grayson says, getting on his bike and handing me a helmet before putting on his own. I stand on the pipes at the back of his bike and hold on to his shoulders as he manoeuvres out of the garage, around the house and out on to the empty road.

We ride along the main road, Grayson peddling

as fast as he can, me looking over my shoulder to make sure we are not being followed. I inhale deeply as Grayson peddles at top speed past the empty fields. Grayson rides over the roundabout then stops the bike abruptly sending me flying forward into his back. He drags his feet on to the ground until we come to a complete stop.

"Why did you do that?" I mumble rubbing my bruised chin. He climbs off the bike.

"Get off," he hisses.

I step off the bike glaring at the back of his head. This boy is so rude! He wheels the bike over to the pavement on the right and peers down the road leading into the town centre. I follow his eyes to see what he's looking at. A man dressed all in black, with a black hood covering his face, is walking through the centre and heading towards us.

My heart skips a beat.

"The Crawler?" I whisper. Grayson nods then spins his bike round.

"That must be why the alarm is going off," he says. "Get on!"

I jump on the back and he peddles away at top speed through the market.

Grayson leans forward, his head between the handlebars, halfway off the seat as he peddles as fast as he can, weaving through the market narrowly missing stalls and empty cartons left on the ground. We stop abruptly at the other end, reappearing on a small windy road I don't recognise. Grayson looks left, then right, even though the road is completely empty. He turns the front wheel and heads down a road lined with warehouses on both sides, then takes a sharp left under a bridge, along a narrow path that leads into some fields. We appear through the long grass at the back of some houses, and it's only then that I recognise that these houses back on to our road.

We jump off Grayson's bike and run along a narrow path between two houses that leads on to our road. Out of breath and panting, I follow him to his house, waiting impatiently as he unlocks the door – we rush inside, closing the door behind us. Only then do we take a deep breath of relief.

Grayson leans on the door to catch his breath, but I walk along the hallway until I am under the stairs. I count the planks *one, two, three,* then get down on my knees. I prise the plank open with my fingers and it moves easily. I peer inside the pitch-black hole.

I can't see anything. I reach inside with my hand feeling around until I touch something. I pull it out. It's a small tin. I open it with Grayson hovering over me. There is a small jar inside labelled MUM. I hand it to Grayson, getting to my feet. He opens it and a strong potent smell fills the air. Grayson shuts it immediately. "Yep, that's it," he says wrinkling his nose.

I slump on the floor finally catching my breath. "There's one thing I don't understand," I say, staring at the white ceiling. Grayson turns his head to look at me.

"If the grandchildren of the Banished were born with magical powers, why don't you have any?"

"The magic only went to the first child," Grayson explains. "That's how it's always been."

I think about this for a few minutes then start to frown. "If everyone in this town is a descendant of the Banished, why did the mayor only banish ten? And why is the Hideaway only for the families of those ten?"

Grayson groans, gets to his feet and walks to the kitchen sink. "You ask a lot of questions," he says, filling his glass with water and gulping it down. He turns to face me and leans against the sink.

"Everyone in this town is a descendant of the original Banished," he explains, "but the mayor only trapped the ones with the strongest magic. The other locals are Norms." He sighs as my brow wrinkles. "Norms are Banished people with limited magical power," he explains. "They have the ability to move objects, or turn water into juice or something." He pulls back the curtains and looks out, "George across the road can change the colour of things with his mind. His dad is always bothering him to change the colour of his car. It's red today, but it was emerald green last week." We both chuckle.

"So the norms are not valuable enough for the Crawler or the mayor," I say.

Grayson's phone pings and he groans, rolling his eyes, "Probably Mum checking on me." He hands me the jar, taking his phone out of his pocket. His eyes scan the phone and his face drains of its colour.

"What is it?" I ask him. He looks up at me and his eyes are wide. "It's from the mayor," he says. "He wants to see you."

I take a step back. "See me?"

Grayson groans inwardly and shakes his head. "This is bad," he mumbles.

I feel a sudden panic rising inside me. "Why does he want to see me?"

"Because he knows," Grayson says sinking on to the floor. "He knows everything."

I sit on the floor across from him, placing the jar next to me. "But how?"

"He has eyes everywhere," Grayson says. "He always knows what's going on."

My throat goes dry. "We should go back to the Hideaway," I say, thinking Mum and Dad will know what to do.

Grayson shakes his head. "We can't lead him there, it's the only place that's protected." He gets to his feet. "We can't hide either, so let's get it over with."

* * * * * * *

We peer through the window to check the coast is clear before sneaking out the front. I spot a neighbour watching us through his window. When I tell Grayson he says everyone locks themselves in their houses when the alarm goes off. "They won't come out until it stops," he explains, "they know it means danger. But the Crawler isn't here for them. He's here for us."

We jump on Grayson's bike and he peddles at full speed down our road. We don't go past the fields this time, instead, he rides down our cul-de-sac to the junction. I look around me worriedly, expecting to see the Crawler.

The wheels of the bike make a buzzing sound as if a hundred bees were making them turn. At the end of the road, Grayson turns left towards the town and I stiffen.

"We can't go that way!" I shout at him from behind.

"We have to," he shouts back, "it's the only way!"

I grip his shoulders tighter the closer to town we get. Ahead, we spot the Crawler still on the high street. He is the only person outside apart from us. He is checking doors and peering through windows. I hold my breath as we get closer. In my head I beg him not to see us, but it's as if I screamed it out loud. The minute it comes into my head, he looks up and spots us.

I squeeze Grayson tightly. "Hurry!" I hiss. The Crawler begins moving towards us, and I think Grayson must be heading straight at him, but then he spins the bike to the right and we disappear down a narrow alley. I look behind me as the Crawler pants, clearly struggling to keep up with us on the bike. I hear shouting, and between gaps of buildings I see him running after us.

I look ahead to the narrow road, at the end are large gates. Grayson fumbles with his phone in one hand, steering the bike with his other. He puts the phone to his ear. "I'm here, I'm here," he says frantically. The gate opens a crack, and we slide through just as it closes behind us. I look over my shoulder, the Crawler is running towards us. Grayson drops the bike on the ground and we run down a stony path lined with tall bushes. We emerge at a brown, one-storey building with a tattered town hall sign above it. I follow Grayson towards the steeple-shaped doors, both of us gasping for air by now. When we reach the doors, Grayson grabs the steel doorknocker and bangs it hard against the door. Within seconds the door opens and we rush inside. A tall man slams it shut behind us; the sound thunders in our ears.

It takes a minute before my breathing slows down and I can finally look around me.

"Follow me," the man grunts. We follow him through a large hall with grey plastic seats piled on top of each other, up three steps to an empty stage and behind the curtain where there is another door. The man unlocks the dark wooden door and leads us down some narrow steps into another room where the mayor sits on a raised platform behind a large oak desk. He leans back in his chair when he sees us, clasping his hands in front of him.

"Ada," he booms. "We meet again."

The mayor beckons us forward with his finger and we oblige, stepping up on to the platform that seems to have no use other than to make him look taller.

"We met on your paper round," he reminds me, which seems friendly enough, except he's not smiling.

I nod. "Yes," I say timidly. He nods as if agreeing with me agreeing with him.

"Sir, the Crawler is here," Grayson interrupts.

"I know," he mutters, tapping his foot on the tiled floor. "Why do you think I raised the alarm?"

He clenches his jaw and leans forward in the leather chair. "What did you find out?" he asks, glancing at Grayson. But before Grayson can answer, the door bursts open and the tall man appears again looking frantic.

"He's broken into the compound," he says.

The mayor's eyes dart around the room, his foot tapping feverishly.

"Do you have a magic spell to get rid of him?" the man asks urgently.

The mayor looks at the man and his face pales. "I burnt it," the mayor says, and he sounds panicked. "I burnt the book of magic so he couldn't steal it. I couldn't risk it falling into his hands. Do you know what it would mean if he got the book? Our lives, the way we live, our freedom would be over."

"Did you make a copy?" the man asks, his voice breaking.

The mayor shakes his head. "No, no," he says. "I didn't have time. I was angry at the Banished for not respecting me and I was afraid of losing it all to him, the Crawler, so I burnt it," he says, sweating profusely.

"So what will we do?" the man asks urgently, looking over his shoulder and up the stairs.

The mayor turns to me. "I know you're one of them. I know you have their magical powers. I saw you in the field. I saw you disappear, and I knew you must have found them. It was the only explanation. Now you must help me."

I look at him horrified. *Help him! I'm just a kid! What can I do against the Crawler? If he's scared, how does he think I feel!*

He grabs my hand suddenly and drags me down the platform with Grayson and the man following behind. At the back of the room, he unlocks a door ushering us in before closing it behind him and bolting it shut. We enter a dark tunnel with dimmed lights against the wall. The mayor rushes down the tunnel not letting go of my hand. We pant as we run, our feet making an echoing sound.

"I had this tunnel built for this very purpose," he explains, out of breath. "So I could get from the town hall to my house without being seen."

"What about the town?" Grayson asks from behind. "Why didn't you build it for all of us, so we could all be safe?" The edge in his voice forces me to steal a glance at him. He's glaring at the back of the mayor's head with such intensity I'm surprised the mayor can't feel it. The mayor doesn't answer.

When we reach the other end of the tunnel, the mayor takes out a bunch of keys from his pocket and opens another door; we enter a living room that could be any living room in this town. It could even be ours.

We rush through the living room, into the hall and out of the front door. It's only then that

I recognise where we are. We are outside the mayor's house. The same house I met him at that first day.

"Go to them," he urges me. "Tell them the town needs their help desperately. Tell them the Crawler is here."

I know exactly who the mayor means by 'them', and so I turn on my heels and run as fast as I can, down his driveway and out on to the road with Grayson close behind. I look to the left frantically, but it is empty, so, with Grayson beside me, I run towards the field, down the embankment and towards the wall of fog.

I take Grayson's hand and run into the fog, but as I enter I realise he is no longer holding my hand.

I look behind me and Grayson is still on the outside, his face baffled as he tries to find me.

I hurry through the fog and out to the other side. There is no one around when I arrive in the Banished kingdom, the town looks deserted. I run between the huts shouting, "Hello?" I rush over to the stone seating but it is empty. I spin around shouting, "Miranda? Caesar?"

Miranda suddenly appears from inside her hut. She runs over, throws her arms around me, and immediately I feel safe.

"Ada," she whispers softly, "am I happy to see you." She calls out behind her, "It's safe. It's Ada." One by one the Banished emerge from their huts, tentatively looking around until they see me and visibly relax.

"We have been hiding," Miranda says leading me over to the seats. "We weren't sure why the alarm was going off, or what might be happening."

She places me in my usual seat in front of the others who all sit around us.

"What's happening out there?" someone shouts.

"Are our families safe?" someone else asks.

Miranda clasps my hand in hers, a line of worry creased into her forehead. "Are they safe, Ada?" she asks softly.

I nod, "Yes, they are in the Hideaway." There is a ripple of relief as everyone sighs. Miranda beams. "That's good," she says. "That's very good." Her smile fades as she looks at me intently, "But you don't seem so happy, Ada," she says.

I take a deep breath summoning all my courage. I never did like talking. Not to anyone. Least of all to a crowd of people. But I have no choice. Things are happening outside, and it is down to me to fix it. I get to my feet. "The Crawler is here," I announce.

There are gasps around the crowd. Shouts of 'No! Not again!' There are so many voices talking I can barely make out what everyone is saying. I hesitate, wonder if I am the right person for this. Why couldn't this gift be given to someone else? Someone louder than me. Someone with more confidence. I feel Miranda's hand in mine and I look down at her. She smiles from her seat, "Speak, Ada," she says. "They will listen."

I twist my spare hand around in circles. "But I'm not loud enough," I tell her.

She squeezes my hand. "They will hear you," she says. "Speak. From your heart."

I face the unsettled crowd, too busy shouting questions to notice I am afraid. My eyes close and I feel a warm wind engulf me. It swirls around me like a protective shield. Behind that wind, in the distance, I see the Crawler running towards me, and in front of him the mayor screaming for help. It is as if this is happening now, but I know it is my mind playing tricks on me. Underground, below the earth, I see Mum, Dad and the others cowering in the Hideaway. I open my eyes, and everyone is silent. Even the trees seem to have stopped moving, it's as if the world has frozen. I have to do this! I have to do what it takes to save them.

"Everyone is safe," I tell them, my voice clear, loud and steady. "But the Crawler is here. The mayor asked for your help. He destroyed the book of magic so the Crawler couldn't steal its secrets, but now the town is helpless. They need you."

The Banished look at me silently, and I feel their eyes piercing through me. One by one they begin to speak. Quietly at first, then louder.

"Why should we help him? He put us here!"

"He doesn't deserve our help, let him rot!"

"But what about our families?" someone shouts, and that someone is me. I take a sharp intake of breath as they fall silent again. "What about your families?" I ask. "What will they do if you won't help them?"

"We will help our families but not him," Caesar shouts.

Miranda stands next to me. "We will help everyone," she replies. She takes my hand, "But we cannot speak through this fog. They cannot hear or see us from the outside and we cannot hear or see them. So you, Ada, you will speak for us."

✦✦ CHAPTER NINE ✦✦

"Wow!" Grayson cries when I reappear. "How did you do that?" I shrug, too busy thinking about what the Banished said.

"So what did they say?" he asks, running to catch up with me.

"They said they will only talk through me," I answer, feeling a sense of urgency and starting to run.

"The mayor won't like that," Grayson says through gasps of breath.

"He doesn't have a choice," I reply firmly. I'm surprised how confident I sound.

The town is still eerily quiet, but I keep a sharp eye on the long road for the Crawler, until we reach the mayor's house and duck into the garden. We hide behind a tall oak tree, waiting until we are both happy that the coast is clear.

"Let's go," Grayson hisses, beckoning me to follow him as we make a dash for the front door.

We knock three times just as the mayor told us to do. The door opens a crack, and the tall man, who Grayson now tells me is the mayor's guard and is called Olson, peers out. When he realises it's us, we are ushered in, and he closes the door quickly behind us.

Olson takes us into the kitchen where the mayor is waiting. It seems so weird when I think about how the Crawler is searching for us and the town is on lockdown, and here is the mayor waiting in his kitchen as though it is just another ordinary day.

"Well?" he jumps to his feet when he sees us. "What did they say?"

"They said they would help," I tell him. The mayor breathes a sigh of relief and glances over at Olson who seems just as relieved.

"Did you tell them I burnt the book of magic? Do they know how to get out?" It seems a silly question. If they knew how to get out, they would have done so already, but this is lost on him.

"Yes, they know you burnt the book," I tell him. "They think there might be another way, but they have a few demands first."

The mayor glares at me as though I have three heads. "Demands?" he chokes, pointing frantically at the wall behind us. "We are under siege! There's no time for demands."

I look at him calmly. After a few seconds he groans and wipes his forehead, "What is it? What do they want?"

I hand him a note Miranda wrote and gave to me before I left her. He unravels it, his eyes scanning the paper. He looks up. "They want to talk through you?"

I nod. He laughs, "You? A child?"

I stiffen, folding my arms against my chest. Wasn't he the same person who asked me for help? Now I'm just a child!

"Well, technically you're already talking through her," Grayson shrugs. He stops abruptly when the mayor shoots him a deadly glare.

We watch as the mayor paces the kitchen, walks the length of it three times, biting the edge of his lip with a deep frown, then stops and looks to Olson with raised eyebrows.

"It's the only way," Olson says.

Suddenly, there is a loud bang on the wall that jolts us. We look at each other urgently.

The Crawler is here.

"Okay, okay," the mayor hisses. "We talk through you. Now what?"

I sigh with relief, turning on my heels, "Follow me."

*. *. *. *. *.

I take the mayor into the Hideaway, but the group seem less than happy to see him. Mr Bell immediately gets to his feet. He shakes his head at me, "This is a safe place for us, you shouldn't have brought him here."

My heart plunges and I lower my eyes to the ground.

The mayor puffs out his chest. "Am I not allowed a safe haven, Jack?" he asks. Mr Bell's face tightens. I pull the mayor to the front of the room while Olson guards the door.

"I've spoken with the Banished," I tell them. "They want to help," I turn to the mayor, "but first you have to tell them what happened to the Banished."

The mayor shifts from one foot to the other, his face sweating. "They know what happened," he says. "They disappeared."

I stare at him. "You have to admit to everything you have done, or the Banished will save everyone but you." I stare at him hard so he understands. The mayor turns to the locals, resting his hands on his hips. He clears his throat, kicking the ground with his feet.

"Well... you know they left us," he says clearing his throat again. He glances at me, "Well, the truth is, I tried to strike a deal with them, to make us the richest town in this country, but they refused."

"What kind of deal?" someone shouted. "Say it." Even though they already know the story, I think they want to hear him say it out loud. They want the mayor to admit to what he did.

The mayor lowers his eyes to the ground, "Well, a deal where they would perform for visitors. People would get their sick healed, or whatever they needed, for a large fee of course. Our town could use the money," he says, suddenly looking around the room at everyone's faces. "We could expand, build a hotel. Jack, your store would be filled out the door. You could sell souvenirs, T-shirts, mugs… "

"Like a circus," Mr Bell says, curling his lip.

The mayor laughs drily, "Well, that's your description Jack. Anyway, they refused, so I took their book of magic and used the Banished's spell against them."

There is an uproar in the room.

"You banished them because they refused to earn you money?" Dad asks in disbelief.

"You are a traitor!" someone cries. "Just like your father!"

The mayor's face tightens and he glares at them. "My father was no traitor," he growls. "He was simply following his best friend to protect him." He turns to me with a sweeping gesture, "But if my father is a traitor, then so is her grandfather."

Dad jumps to his feet. "My father is no traitor," Dad says through clenched teeth – I have never seen him so angry.

The crowd erupts again shouting at the mayor who looks to me, his foot tapping. "So, what now? Now you've thrown me to the wolves?"

I say nothing, my heart pounding hard against my chest. *What have I done?*

It's late when we all make an effort to get some sleep. Mr and Mrs Pillock hand out blankets to everyone and we find a space on the floor to lie down.

"The Crawler won't find us unless someone leads him here," Mr Bell says, shooting a look at the mayor.

"Now, why would I do that Jack?" the mayor asks, throwing his hands up in frustration.

Mum finds a corner and calls me and Dad over. She hands me and Dad blankets to spread out. Dad lies on his back with his hands behind his head.

"Well, when I woke up this morning, I didn't think we would be hiding from the Crawler while waiting for magic people to save us," he says. He turns his head towards Mum, "Did you?"

Mum shakes her head with a heavy sigh.

"Told you not to move from the city," I mumble. They both look at me in silence before Dad starts chuckling, his stomach rising and falling, which makes me and Mum laugh too.

Someone turns the light out and we are plunged into darkness.

"So what's the plan my little hero?" Dad whispers in the dark. I copy him, lying on my back with my hands behind my head. I'm wondering the same thing. What is next? Before I left Miranda, she said to wait for a sign but I'm afraid I might have missed it. I wriggle into a comfy spot preparing to stay awake all night, but within minutes I am fast asleep.

In my dream, I am sitting on the familiar stone seat, facing the Banished. I feel a warm breeze brush my skin and Miranda stands in front of me. She lays her hands on my arms; they are warm like a summer's day when the sun hits your skin.

"Ada," she says softly, "you have the power to bring us home."

I look at her wide-eyed. "How?"

She smiles gently, "You can see and hear things no one else can. That is one of your magical powers."

"But how will that help you?" I ask, confused. She takes my hands in hers and squeezes them. "You just have to believe."

I wake with a jolt and sit upright. My breathing is shallow as I look around me expecting to see the Banished. The room is deathly quiet except for the mayor snoring like a train.

I stare at my hands as my eyes get used to the dark. I notice something on my right palm. The word 'believe' appears in the palm of my hand as though someone is writing it as I watch.

My heart skips a beat. I look around me but no one is awake. I remember Miranda's words to look out for a sign.

This must be it. This must be my sign.

I cross my legs, resting my hands on my knees and close my eyes. Maybe what I dreamt wasn't a dream after all. Maybe Miranda was really speaking to me. I take a deep breath and try to think of the Banished. I try to remember their faces but all I can see is Miranda urging me on.

"You can do it, Ada," she whispers. Her voice is so clear it's as if she is right beside me. I squeeze my eyes tighter. I see her, clear as day, the long, flowing white

85

dress she wears, the green locs that fall to her back. Her warm smile. I reach for her hand and it's soft, just like I remember it.

"Ada… Ada." I stir. Her voice is so clear. So real. "Ada, open your eyes." I open my eyes to see Miranda knelt down beside me, a glow of light surrounding her. I jump up, startled. She lays a hand on my shoulder.

"You did it," she says smiling. "You brought me here."

I look around me, everyone else is still sleeping.

"Only you can see and hear me," she explains, standing. "Come dear Ada, it's time."

I follow her, stepping over the sleeping people while she floats over them like a ghost. She turns to me as we reach the door.

"Ada, use your magical power to take us outside." I squeeze my eyes shut as tight as I can, then open them. We are still in the Hideaway.

"I can't," I whisper.

Miranda takes my face in her hands. "Yes, you can," she says firmly. "This is your power, Ada. This is how you learn. Close your eyes and imagine a spot outside. See it in your mind and take us there."

I nod and close my eyes again. I try to remember what the outside of Mr Pillock's garage looks like, how it sits behind his house and there are two bins to the side, a fence to the right.

I feel my body lift and when I open my eyes we are standing outside. I gasp, "How did you do that?"

"How did *you* do that," she corrects me. "Everything you do from now on, Ada, is all you. I am just here to guide you. To help you find your true strength."

I follow her along the path outside Mr and Mrs Pillock's house. "So, are you free from the fog?" I ask.

Miranda looks over her shoulder at me and laughs softly, "No, we are not free. Only you can see the fog, only you can see and speak to us. We didn't know this was possible until we saw it with our own eyes."

"Why can I see that fog?" I ask.

"Well, we have wondered the same thing," she says. "Our only guess is that you have always had the magic inside you, you just never realized. If we knew who you are a descendant of, we might know what your true power is. "

I lower my eyes to avoid hers. "My grandfather," I tell her, "is Amron."

Miranda stops in her tracks but I dare not look at her. I feel her hand on my shoulder. "Ada," I raise my eyes to look at her and her smile is soft. "What Mocasa did has nothing to do with you or your grandfather. Amron was a good man. A true leader."

"You're not mad?" I whisper.

She shakes her head, wrapping her arm around my shoulder as we continue to walk. "I could never be mad at you, Ada," she says. "You are saving our lives."

My heart feels suddenly heavy. What if I can't save them? What if I'm not the person they think I am?

I think about this for some time as we enter the main road with only the moon and a few streetlamps to guide us.

"I was always like this?" I mumble.

Miranda stops and looks up and down the road. She turns to face me. "Ada, listen to me, this is very important. You need to summon all of us here to help you."

I frown, "Help me do what?"

She is about to answer, when her body stiffens and her eyes widen. "He's here," she says, "I can feel him." She turns slowly and in the distance the Crawler is

88

heading towards us. Miranda turns back to face me, this time her expression is frantic. She takes my face in her hands. "Ada, summon us... NOW!"

I stare at her frightened. "I don't know how."

"You do, you do!" she says urgently as I look over her shoulder at the Crawler getting closer. "Don't look at him. Close your eyes and focus. Just like you did inside the Hideaway when you summoned me. Just like you did when you brought us outside. This is not the way I wanted you to learn, Ada, but we have no choice. You must learn, now."

I squeeze my eyes shut but all I can hear is the sound of the Crawler getting closer.

Miranda leans in towards my ear, "Focus, Ada," her voice sounds loud like a storm. I squeeze my eyes tighter, clenching my fists.

I wish the Banished were here. I wish Miranda and Caesar, Doris, Shah, Clay, Ruman, Elis, Abo, Fawn, Boa, were all here, behind me, like a wall, protecting me. I see them in my head as clear as day. I clench my fists tightly, breathing fast and heavy. *Please!* I beg them. *Help us!* I feel their hands on my shoulders, their breath as though they were right behind me. I hear their voices. I feel a sudden chill. I open my eyes slowly and breathlessly look behind me. They are here! All of them, in the flesh. Caesar winks at me.

"You did it," he whispers before looking above my head, his smile fading. Someone pulls me back, and the Banished step forward in a line in front of me.

They extend their hands towards the Crawler, opening and closing their hands in perfect unison. There is a roar of thunder and the ground shakes beneath us. I put my arms out to steady myself, fear gripping my whole body. Bolts of lightning flash from all ends of the sky, meeting in the middle and forming a ball. The Banished suddenly pull their hands back to their shoulders, their palms facing outwards controlling the ball of lightning.

"NOW!" Miranda roars. They throw their hands forward shooting the ball of lightning in the direction of the Crawler.

From behind the Banished, I hear shouting. Then suddenly the ball of lightning rises. It twists and turns in the sky with the Crawler kicking and screaming inside. I gasp as the ball of lightning hovers, held steady by the Banished, then with a sudden shoot of their hands, it disappears and we are plunged into darkness again.

I push through the crowd to see where the Crawler has gone, but the road is empty, like it never happened. "Where did he go?" I gasp.

Miranda places an arm around me. "He will find himself a couple of hundred miles out of town, disorientated and forgetful. He won't remember who we, or Littleton, are."

"So it's over?" I ask.

Miranda gives a slight tilt of her head. "Well, we will need to cast a spell to protect the town so no one can do this again, but yes, it's over." She kisses my head. "You have saved us, Ada. You saved us and you saved our town."

When we return to the Hideaway, I turn the light on waking everyone. One by one they open their eyes. Grayson is the first to see the Banished. "Caesar!" he shouts, jumping to his feet and throwing himself at his brother. There are gasps around the room, then shouting and crying as the Banished run to their loved ones. Mum and Dad make their way over to me as we watch everyone reunite.

"You did this, Ada?" Dad asks in awe.

I nod my head. "Miranda helped me, she showed me my magical powers, but the Banished got rid of the Crawler."

"The Crawler is gone?" the mayor cries, overhearing me. Miranda pulls away from Mr Bell, her father, who has tears in his eyes.

"It's true. The Crawler is gone," she announces and the room erupts in cheers. Miranda waves her hand towards me, "But the thanks go to Ada, who learnt her magic in record time, and saved us."

Everyone turns to me, beaming. Grayson lets go of his brother and runs over throwing his arms around me. "Thanks, Ada," he whispers. "Sorry for thinking you were weird when you first arrived."

I pull back narrowing my eyes, "You thought I was weird? *You* were the weird one following me on your bike!"

Miranda tells us we should let the rest of the town know that all is clear, and as we leave the Hideaway, Grayson and I continue arguing about our first impressions of each other.

We emerge outside and Miranda finds me, linking her arm with mine.

"You and I have a unique bond now, Ada," she says. "It's one that no one but we will understand. We are connected for life."

"What will happen to the mayor?" I ask.

Miranda sighs, "Well, I think his mayor days are over. There are many changes to be made. Finally we seem to have moved away from our past, and now, we look to the future. But first," she says squeezing my shoulder, "first, we rest, then we can start planning the future we have always wanted. One with peace."

As we all head down the road towards our homes the sun begins to rise to a new day. I glance over my shoulder towards the field and let out a sigh of relief – the fog is gone. It really is over.

READING ZONE!

QUIZ TIME

Can you remember the answers to these questions?

- How does Ada feel about her paper round on the first morning she has to wake up?

- Who has a really old car outside his house?

- What did Ada expect to see when she walked through the fog?

- What is the name of the place the Banished would hide their families to protect them and how do you get to it?

- What did the mayor do to the book of magic and why?

READING ZONE!

STORYTELLING TOOLKIT

The story is set in both the real world and a world of magic. How does the author introduce us to the two worlds?

Think about the descriptions of the town Ada and her family move to and of the people who live there. When Ada first steps into the fog, how do we find out that it is a new world?

READING ZONE!

GET CREATIVE

Imagine you could step through fog and enter a new world. Can you write a paragraph describing the world you emerge into? What would you see, hear and smell? How would feel? What would the people be like?

When you have written your description, draw a picture of the scene you have described.